HE'S NOT MY DOG

Books by the same author

DYAN SHELDON

Illustrations by Kate Sheppard

WALKER BOOKS
AND SUBSIDIARIES
LONDON · BOSTON · SYDNEY · AUCKLAND

For Floyd and for Pepe

First published 2001 by Walker Books Ltd
87 Vauxhall Walk, London SE11 5HJ

4 6 8 10 9 7 5 3

Text © 2001 Dyan Sheldon
Illustrations © 2001 Kate Sheppard

This book has been typeset in Plantin

Printed and bound by J. H. Haynes & Co. Ltd

British Library Cataloguing in Publication Data:
a catalogue record for this book
is available from the British Library

ISBN 0-7445-5972-3

Contents

Chapter One

Every Sunday I went to football practice. There was a newsagent's near the bus stop, and if I didn't see a bus coming I'd nip in for a chocolate bar or a packet of crisps to get me through the ride.

I'd seen the dog outside the shop before. He was just a black and white short-haired mutt, with a patch over one eye. He looked like he should be running around chasing sheep. Usually he was tied up to the bubble gum machine, but this Sunday he wasn't. He was just sitting with his back to the door, staring at the road.

He stood up and wagged his tail as soon as he saw me. I gave him a pat and went inside.

There was no one else in the shop, so I didn't have to queue like I usually did. The dog wagged his tail again when I came back out. He looked really sad.

"What's the matter, boy?" I rubbed his head. "Did your owner forget about you?"

He didn't jump up at me, or lick me, or anything like that. He just kept gazing at me as if he didn't have a friend in the world.

The bus came just then, so I gave him another quick pat and made a run for it.

The bus was a double-decker. I like

them better than the one-level buses. I always sit on top if there's room. My favourite seat is the one right at the front. Even things you've seen a thousand times before look different from up there. And sometimes you think the bus is going to tilt over, or crash into something. It makes the ride more interesting.

I reckoned it was my lucky day. Not only had the newsagent's been empty, but the front seat on the top deck was free.

I settled in and started to unwrap my chocolate bar.

"Child's fare," I told the conductor when she came by.

She handed me the ticket. "You know," she said, "you'll have to keep that dog out of the aisle. That's the rule."

I reckoned I must have misheard her.

"Pardon?" I smiled so she'd know I wasn't being rude. "I'll have to do what?"

"The dog," she repeated. "You'll have to keep the dog out of the aisle."

I looked down. The black and white dog from in front of the newsagent's was practically sitting on her feet. He was staring at the chocolate in my hand as if he hadn't eaten for a week.

I gave the conductor another smile. "He's not my dog," I told her.

"Of course he isn't." She sighed. "Just keep him out of the aisle."

Chapter Two

Because he kept staring at me with his sad face, I gave the dog half my chocolate bar. After he was sure there wasn't so much as a crumb left, he went to sleep under my seat.

When we came to my stop, I got up very quietly so I didn't wake him. Then I ran like mad down the stairs and jumped off the bus before he had time to realize I was gone. I didn't think Mr Douglas would be too happy if I turned up to football practice with a dog. Mr Douglas, our coach, had rules.

I was waiting to cross the road to

the park beside a girl with bright blue hair. That's why I noticed her, because of the hair. I heard the girl say something about a nice dog, but I thought she was talking to the girl who was with her, whose hair was green.

"What's his name?" asked the girl.

I looked over. She was leaning down, patting the black and white dog. He was gazing at her as though she was a delicious meal that no one was going to let him eat. She was looking at me.

"I don't know," I said. "He's not my dog."

The dog licked my hand. He probably thought there was still some chocolate on my fingers.

"Really?" She laughed. "He looks like he's your dog."

I stuck my hand in my pocket. "Yeah," I said, "but he's not."

The lights changed then and the girl, her friend and I all started across the road. The dog came too.

The girl laughed again. "Maybe you'd better tell him he's not with you," she said.

Mr Douglas spotted the dog straight away. I was right about his rules.

"What's that, Andre?" he shouted. "We can't have dogs on the field during practice. You know better than that."

"He's not my dog," I said. "He followed me."

"Well, tell him to go away," said Mr Douglas. "And hurry up. You're late.

We're ready to start."

"Go away," I said to the dog. I gave him a gentle shove. "Shoo!"

The dog didn't budge. He just stared at me with his sad, brown eyes. He reminded me of Bambi, if you reckon that Bambi smelled like old socks.

I gave him another shove. "Go away," I ordered. "I've got stuff to do."

The way he was looking at me, I felt like I was throwing him out of a cosy house on a stormy night, not begging him to get off the pitch.

"Andre!" bawled Mr Douglas. "We haven't got all day!"

I dragged the dog all the way back to the park entrance by his collar, and ran to join the others. I looked over once before we started to play, but I reckoned he'd given up because I couldn't see him any more.

I was streaming down the field with the ball when Rick Neyland tackled me. I went down like a felled tree.

I was still on the ground when Rick started shouting. "Cut it out!" he screamed. "Somebody get him off!"

I looked round. The black and white dog had hold of Rick's shorts and was pulling him away from me.

Mr Douglas came tearing towards us, blowing his whistle. "Andre!" he roared. "Andre, what did I tell you about that dog?"

"Tell him to let go!" Rick was screaming. "He's going to rip my shorts!"

I grabbed hold of the collar again,

and pulled. The dog started licking my face while I tried to explain again to Mr Douglas that he wasn't my dog.

Mr Douglas didn't believe me. "Next time, leave him at home," he said. "Or you can stay at home yourself."

Chapter Three

After practice I went over to my friend Chung's.

The dog followed me back to the bus stop, but by now this didn't surprise me. This time, I was prepared.

The dog and I got on the bus together. He went straight up the stairs, as if he knew that was where I always sat. When all I could see was the tip of his tail, I raced back down and jumped off the bus as it pulled out into the road.

I took the next bus that came along. I was feeling pretty pleased with myself until we passed the newsagent's where

I'd bought my bar of chocolate. The black and white dog was sitting by the door, staring at the road as though he was waiting for someone. I swear he looked up at the bus and right into my eyes. I looked away, feeling a bit like I'd shot Bambi.

But I forgot about the dog once I got to Chung's. Chung had a new computer game, and we spent the rest of the afternoon playing with that and mucking about.

Chung's mother came home around teatime. She stuck her head in the door. "Andre," she said, "you can bring the dog inside, you know. He looks so lonely out there on his own."

Chung said, "What dog?"

I was pretty sure I knew what dog.

"He's not my dog," I told her. "I don't know whose he is."

"Really?" She shook her head the way she had the time Chung and I made popcorn and forgot to put a lid on the pan and got it all over the kitchen. "Well, you can bring him in if you like," said Chung's mother.

Chapter Four

I decided to leave Chung's by the back
door so the dog didn't see me. It
meant climbing over the wall and
going through the neighbour's garden,
but I reckoned it was better than the
dog following me home. I'd never get
rid of him once he knew where I lived.
Mr Douglas wasn't the only adult in
my life who had rules. My mother
would go mad if I brought a dog
home. She'd banned all pets after I
drowned my turtle, even though it was
an accident. My mother said it showed
I wasn't responsible enough to take
care of another creature.

Chung's neighbour yelled at me from his kitchen window. "You!" he bellowed. "What d'you think you're doing? Get out of my garden!"

"I'm sorry!" I shouted back. "I just—" I backed into a rake and it banged me on the head.

"Look what you're doing!" screamed Chung's neighbour. "Get out of my garden now!"

I apologized again. "I'm really sorry. I was just taking a short cut."

My apology didn't exactly impress him. "Next time take your short cut through someone else's garden!"

All the time I was talking, I was backing down the alleyway. That's how I tripped over the hose. I more or less fell onto the pavement.

Even lying flat on the ground I could see the dog at the end of the road. He was sitting at the corner, but he stood up as soon as he saw me land.

He trotted over and started licking me. I was too shaken to push him off. I tried reasoning instead.

"Look," I said. "I've got to go home, and you've got to go home too."

He wagged his tail and rubbed his nose against my face. I tried not to think about germs.

"No," I said. "Not with me. You've got to go to *your* home."

He must have got the message, because he stopped licking and rubbing and gave me his I-am-the-saddest-dog-in-the-world look. It was enough to break your heart. But I was pretty certain it wouldn't break my mother's heart.

"Be reasonable," I pleaded. "I don't even like dogs that much."

He hung his head.

That's when I finally noticed the tag on his collar. It was flat and silver. I got up and limped over to the street light, dragging him with me. The tag had his name on it and a phone number. His name was Floyd.

"What sort of name is that for a dog?" I asked him.

He pressed his nose against my hand.

Floyd and I stopped at the first phone box we came to. It only took cards. We walked to the next phone box. This one took coins, but it wouldn't take mine.

I was feeling pretty hungry by then, so I bought a bag of chips at the fish shop. I sat on the kerb to eat them while I thought about what to do. Floyd was hungry too. He didn't even mind the vinegar or the salt.

"Slow down," I warned him. "Don't forget to chew."

He looked like he was sorry, but he didn't slow down much. I was still hungry after the chips were gone.

I finally managed to get a dialling tone at the next phone box. I punched in the number on Floyd's tag.

The phone was disconnected.

Floyd rested his chin against my knee as if he'd known all along that there wouldn't be any answer. They're

not there, are they? his big brown eyes
seemed to be saying. I'm all alone.

I patted his head. "They probably
moved without telling you."

It made sense to me.

That's when it started to rain.

Chapter Five

I didn't see that I had much choice
about what to do with Floyd. I
couldn't very well leave him out in the
rain, could I? He might catch cold or
something. Besides, as far as I knew,
all he'd had to eat all day was part of
a chocolate bar and the better half of
a bag of chips. If that was all I'd had
all day I'd be starving. That's why I
decided to take him home. Quietly, so
my mum wouldn't notice. I reckoned
he could stay in the garden shed,
where he'd be dry and my mother
would never know he was there.

My mother was sitting on the sofa

reading as Floyd and I came up to the house. I could see her through the living-room window. She looked up and waved. I waved back. Because Floyd didn't quite reach my knee, my mum wouldn't be able to see him unless she actually stood up. I grabbed hold of his collar as soon as I opened the front door, and then I yanked him down the hall to the kitchen without pausing for breath.

Floyd liked the kitchen. His head went up and he started sniffing the air. He didn't look any happier, but he was definitely interested in the smells. There was spaghetti sauce simmering on the stove.

As quietly as possible, I opened the garden door. "Come on, Floyd,"

I whispered.

I'd had to let go of his collar to get the key, and Floyd had gone back to sit by the refrigerator, his nose pointed towards the pot on the front burner.

"Floyd!" I hissed. "Come on!"

Floyd gazed back at me as if he was a picture that was painted on the door of the fridge.

I had to do the yanking-him-along-by-his-collar routine again, but this time Floyd refused to help. He locked his legs and dug his claws in. He was heavier than he looked. I felt like I was dragging a bag of cement across the floor.

Floyd finally moved when we got to the back door. He took one look at the rain and spread his legs so he had a foot on each side of the frame. I couldn't pull him through.

"You watch too many films," I whispered. "Dogs don't do things like this."

Floyd gazed back at me sadly.

I tugged as hard as I could, but he wouldn't budge.

There was nothing for it. I was going to have to carry Floyd to the garden shed.

"Andre!" my mother called from the front room. "Andre, are you in the kitchen?"

I wasn't technically in the kitchen just then, I was out on the patio trying to get my arms round Floyd, but I shouted back "Yes!"

"Put the water on for the pasta,

will you?"

"OK," I grunted.

It wasn't until I got him in my arms
that I realized, stretched out, Floyd
was nearly as tall as I was. I had his
nose in my face and his claws pressed
against my thighs. His front paws were
fastened to my shoulders. He was
looking at me as if he'd just had the
idea that I might be mad.

"You're going to love the shed," I
told him as I carefully turned round.
"It's really cool."

I didn't look left or right as Floyd
and I staggered down the garden path.
I was too busy praying. Praying that
none of our neighbours would see me.
Praying that my mother would stay on
the sofa. Praying that I wouldn't drop

Floyd, or stumble over something in the dark.

It seemed to take hours, but at last we reached the shed.

"I hope you appreciate all I'm doing for you," I gasped as I set Floyd down.

Floyd licked my nose and looked round. I could tell from the expression on his face that he didn't like the shed half as much as he liked the kitchen.

"It'll be fine," I said in my most reassuring voice. "Trust me."

Floyd put his paw on my knee. I took this as a yes.

The garden shed was damp and falling apart, but it was the one place my mother never went. I found a box and an old blanket, and I made Floyd a bed under the broken barbecue. I stretched an old shower curtain over it to keep him dry. Floyd watched me with his sad eyes. Why are you doing this to me? he seemed to be saying. Why can't I stay inside with you?

When I had finished, I pointed out the hole at the side of the shed that was big enough for him to get through if he wanted to go out.

"You'll be all right here," I told him. He liked being patted. "I'll come back later with some food."

He stared at me patiently. No, you won't. You'll leave me, like everyone else…

"I will," I promised. "I'll bring you something really good."

Chapter Six

After supper I offered to do the washing-up.

My mother looked at me like she thought I might have the flu. "What's got into you?" she asked suspiciously.

"Nothing." I shrugged. "You work hard all week. You deserve a day off."

"Well…" said my mum. I could tell she was choosing between going back to her book and ringing the doctor.

"You go and relax." I gave her a sympathetic smile. "I'll bring you a cup of tea."

Looking slightly dazed, my mother went back to the living-room.

I got some food together for Floyd while the kettle was boiling. I filled a bowl with some of the leftover pasta. There was an old slice of pizza and a couple of cooked sausages in the fridge, so I took them too, and half of my pudding that I'd saved from supper. Floyd didn't look any happier when he saw the food, but he still scoffed the lot.

My mother looked up when I brought her the tea.

"What happened to you?" she wanted to know.

I glanced down at my jeans to see if there were any black and white dog hairs on them, but I couldn't see anything.

"Nothing."

"Your hair looks wet," said my mother.

I'd worn my jacket when I went to feed Floyd, and I'd taken off my shoes as soon as I got back inside, but I'd forgotten about my head.

"Does it?"

She gave me a curious look. "Yes, it does."

I laughed. "It must be from the washing-up," I said. "You know, splashing all that water about."

My mother picked up her cup. "You're not meant to hose them down," she said. "They're dishes, not elephants."

I lay awake that night, listening to the rain and worrying about Floyd. Even when I finally fell asleep, I dreamed about him. We were playing football in the park together. Floyd didn't look any happier in my dream than he did in real life, but he was an excellent goalie.

The sun was shining when I woke up. I got dressed while my mum was still in the bathroom and sneaked into the garden. Floyd wasn't in the shed. The water and broken biscuits I'd left in case he got hungry in the night had gone, and so had he.

My mother thought I was getting a cold.

"You seem a bit down," she said over breakfast. "Are you sure you're all right?"

"Yeah," I said. "I'm fine. I'm just

tired. The rain kept me awake."

Which was almost true.

But when I got to the corner of our road, there was Floyd, waiting for me. He gave me a sad but hopeful look.

"Well, how was I supposed to know you'd be here?" I asked. "If I'd known, I would have brought you something to eat."

He looked so unhappy I almost thought he was going to cry.

"Stop making me feel guilty," I ordered.

He didn't stop. He just looked at me like I'd really let him down. I gave him half my lunch, and then we had to run all the way to school.

Mr Blakely, the caretaker, was in the playground. "You know the rules,

Andre!" he shouted when he saw us.
"No dogs allowed."

"He's not my dog," I shouted back.
I hurried towards the entrance, Floyd
on my heels.

"He seems to be with you," said Mr
Blakely.

"He's not. He's not my dog."

Mr Blakely clapped his hands.
"Shoo! Shoo!" he yelled at Floyd.

Floyd just stared back at him sadly,
but it didn't work with Mr Blakely. He
stamped his foot and shouted "Shoo!
Shoo!" again.

While Mr Blakely was keeping Floyd
busy, I raced through the door and
shut it behind me.

Floyd was waiting at the gate when I

came out that afternoon.

Unfortunately, my mother was
waiting there too. I'd totally forgotten
that she was meant to be taking me
shopping.

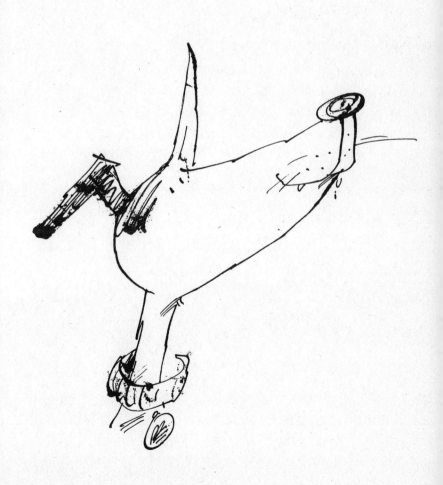

Chapter Seven

My mother didn't notice Floyd until
we came out of the shop with my new
football boots.

"Wasn't that dog there when we
went in?" she asked.

I swung the carrier bag between us.
"What dog?"

"That dog," said my mum. She
stared at Floyd as though she was
trying to remember where they first
met. Floyd stared sadly back at her.
"Wasn't he at the school?"

"I don't think so," I said. "There are
a lot of dogs who look like that."

My mother looked round. "Well,

who does he belong to?"

"Don't ask me," I said. "He's not my dog, that's for sure."

We stopped at the butcher's shop on the way home. One of the butchers leaned over the counter while my mother was paying at the till.

"Andre!" he whispered. "I put some bones in the bag." He winked. "For the dog."

I looked towards the front of the shop. Floyd was at the window, staring in between the chicken legs with his big Bambi eyes.

"He's not my dog," I whispered back.

The butcher winked again. "I'll have more for him next time," he promised.

* * *

Because I hadn't slept much the night before, I was pretty tired by the time I got to bed. Floyd almost looked happy when I gave him his bones, so I didn't have to worry about him. And my mother didn't suspect there was a dog in the garden shed, so I wasn't worried about her either. I fell into a deep sleep.

I dreamed I was in prison. I was trying to dig my way out with a spoon, but the guards heard the noise. A searchlight fell on me—

I sat up in bed. I could still hear the sound of digging.

I got out of bed and went to the window. It was a clear night, with a sky full of stars and a fat white moon.

What I could see of Floyd was his

bottom. His tail was sticking straight out like a flag. He was digging a hole under a shrub in a corner of the garden.

My mother's room was at the front of the house, which was both a good thing and a bad thing. It was a good thing because it meant she wouldn't hear the digging. It was a bad thing because to get downstairs I had to walk past her door. I could hear her radio playing faintly, which meant she was still awake. My mother has the hearing of a bat. There was no way I could get downstairs without her knowing.

That's why I decided to climb out on the tree. I reckoned I could get Floyd's attention from there and tell him to stop digging up my mother's garden. The tree was right outside my window and I'd climbed it about a trillion times before, so I didn't think there would be any problem.

I was almost right.

There was no problem getting out. I crawled out along one of the biggest branches till I could see Floyd just below me. He was burying a bone.

"Floyd!" I hissed. "Floyd!"

Floyd raised his head. There was dirt on his snout and a bone in his mouth.

"Get back in the shed!" I ordered. "Right now!"

Floyd cocked his head to one side. He couldn't work out where I was.

I crawled a little further along.

"Floyd!" I called again. "Floyd! Go

back inside!"

This time I knew he'd seen me, because he stood up against the trunk of the tree and started wagging his tail.

I hadn't counted on this. Not only was there no way Floyd was going to go back in the shed now that he'd seen me in the tree, but there was a chance that he might start barking.

"Wait there!" I commanded. "I'm coming down!"

I reckoned I could reach the wall and jump to the ground from there.

And I could have done it too – if my mother hadn't had the tree pruned. Unfortunately, I forgot about the pruning until I reached for a branch that wasn't there any more.

Floyd began to moan softly.

Everything that goes up must come down, but not everything that comes down can get back up. I couldn't. I was so far out on the branch that the one above me was out of reach. I tried to crawl back towards the trunk and nearly slipped off.

Floyd started jumping at the tree.

"Calm down!" I whispered. "This may take some time."

But the branches that would have helped me get to the wall were the same ones that would have helped me get back to my room, and they were gone. I was going to need more than some time to get out of the tree – I was going to need a couple of firemen as well.

"It's no use," I told Floyd. "I'm stuck."

Floyd gazed at me for a few seconds, and then he sat down. He leaned his head back and began to howl.

Floyd's a really good howler. If I hadn't been watching him, I would have sworn there was a coyote in our back garden.

A few dozen other people must have thought there was a coyote in our back garden though, because lights started going on in all the neighbouring houses.

And then my bedroom light went on and my mother appeared at the window. She looked at me, and then down at Floyd.

"Isn't that the dog that followed us to the shoe shop and the butcher's?" she asked.

I smiled as though this were a perfectly reasonable question to ask someone who was stuck up a tree in the middle of the night. "Yeah," I said. "I think he must have followed us home."

My mother got the ladder and waited with Floyd while I climbed down.

"Are you all right?" she asked when I reached the ground.

"Yeah," I said. "I'm fine."

Floyd was so glad to see me, he nearly knocked me over. He was jumping up and down with happiness.

"Just whose dog is this?" asked my mother.

"He's not mine," I said, trying to push him off me.

"Well, whose is he?" my mother asked again.

I explained how Floyd had followed me to football practice. I explained trying to ring the number on his tag. I even explained about the shed and the butcher and everything.

"Well," said my mother when I had finished. "We can't stand out here all night. We'd better go back to bed."

Floyd and I both looked at her.

"You too," she said to Floyd. "But you're not allowed on Andre's bed."

I couldn't believe my ears. "But you said I couldn't have a dog!"

"I said you couldn't have another pet until you learned some responsibility, but it sounds to me as if you've been taking very good care of Floyd." She sighed. "And besides, he may not be your dog, but you certainly seem to be his boy." She patted Floyd's head. "Isn't that right?"

Floyd licked her hand, and then he turned his eyes on me.

Maybe it was the dark, but for a second it really looked to me like he was smiling.

LEON LOVES BUGS
Dyan Sheldon

Leon loves bugs. He loves to trap them, make them race, and stomp on their homes. Leon just can't leave bugs alone. What Leon needs is to see things from a different point of view…

TOM AND THE PTEROSAUR
Jenny Nimmo

Tom's got a secret – and it's out of this world!

At the bottom of the Tuttle family's garden rises a huge hedge, as tall and as solid as the wall of a castle.

Behind it live the Grimleys, but what they're trying to hide no one knows. Then one evening Tom Tuttle hears an eerie wailing. What sort of creature could make such a noise – a noise that stops when Tom's sisters sing? And if he uncovers the truth, will anyone believe him?

Discover the answers in this intriguing story by a Smarties Book Prize-winning author.

"Go away."
I gave him a
gentle shove.
"Shoo!"

Andre often sees the black and
white dog sitting patiently
outside the newsagent's. But one
Sunday morning, Andre gets
a surprise: the dog follows him
onto the bus. He follows
him off the bus. He follows
him to football practice. He
follows Andre home. "He's not
my dog," Andre tells everyone.
But no one believes him.
Especially not the dog!

Cover illustration by Kate Sheppard

£3.99
UK ONLY

ISBN 0-7445-5972-3

9 780744 559729